THE MAN WHO DIDN'T WASH HIS DISHES

By Phyllis Krasilovsky

Illustrated by Barbara Cooney

SCHOLASTIC INC.
New York Toronto London Auckland Sydney

ISBN 0-590-44678-9

12 11 10 9 8 7 6 5 4 3   3 4 5 6/9

Printed in the U.S.A.   23

To the one and only
Thomas Finney, with love

There once was a man who lived all alone
in a little house on the edge of a town.
He didn't have any wife or children,
so he always cooked his own supper,
cleaned the house by himself,
and made his own bed.

One night he came home hungrier
than usual, so he made himself
a big, big supper.

It was a very good supper
(he liked to cook and could make
good things to eat),
but there was so much of it
that he grew very, very tired
by the time he'd finished.

He just sat back in his chair,
as full as he could be, and decided
he'd leave the dishes in the sink
till the next night, and then
he would wash them all at once.

But the next night
he was TWICE as hungry,
so he cooked TWICE as big a supper,
and took TWICE as long to eat it,
and was TWICE as tired by the time
he'd finished.

So he left THOSE dishes in the sink too.

Well, as the days went by, he
got hungrier and hungrier, and
more and more tired, and so he
never washed his dishes.

After a while there were so MANY
dirty dishes that they didn't
all fit in the sink. So he began
to pile them on the table.

Soon the table was so full that he
began to put them on his bookshelves.

And when THEY were full,
he put them just everywhere he could find
an empty place.

Soon he had them piled on the floor too.

In fact, the floor got to be so FULL of dishes

that he had a hard time
getting into his house at night —
THEY WERE EVEN PILED
AGAINST THE DOOR!

Then one night he looked in
his closet and found that there
WASN'T ONE CLEAN DISH LEFT!
He was hungry enough
to eat out of anything,
so he ate out of the soap dish
from the bathroom. It was too dirty
for him to use again the NEXT night,
so he used one of his ash trays.

Pretty soon he had used up
all the ash trays. THEN
he ate out of some clean
flowerpots he found down
in the cellar. When THEY
were all used up, he ate
out of candy dishes and
drank water from vases.

Finally he used up EVERYTHING —
even the pots he cooked his food in —
and he didn't know what to do!
He was SOOOO unhappy!

His whole house was full of dirty dishes
— and dirty flowerpots
— and dirty ash trays
— and dirty candy dishes
— and dirty pots
— and a dirty soap dish.

He couldn't find his books
— or his alarm clock
— or even his BED any more!

He couldn't sit down to think because
even his chairs were filled with dishes,
and he couldn't find the sink
so he could wash them!

But THEN—all of a sudden
IT BEGAN TO RAIN!

And the man got an idea.

He drove his big truck around to the side
of the house and piled all the dishes on it
—and all the vases
—and all the flowerpots
—and all the ash trays
—and all the candy dishes
—and the soap dish,
and drove the truck
out into the rain.

The rain fell on everything,
and soon all the things were clean again.
THE RAIN HAD WASHED THEM!

Then the man carried everything back into the house.

He put the dishes in the dish closet,
the pots in the pot closet,
the ash trays on the tables,
the candy dishes on the shelves,
the flowerpots in the cellar,
the vases in their places,
and the soap dish in the bathroom.

He was so very, very tired after carrying everything back and putting it away that he decided from then on he would always wash his dishes just as soon as he had finished his supper.

The next night when he came home he cooked his supper, and when he had finished eating it, he washed the dishes and put them right away. And he did this every night after that.

The man is very happy now. He can find his chairs, and he can find his alarm clock, and he can find his bed. It is easy for him to get into his house too, because there are no more dishes piled on the floor — or anywhere!